A TALE AS TALL AS JACOB

MISADVENTURES WITH MY BROTHER

SAMANTHA EDWARDS

TO JACOB, LUKE, AND GRACE:
THANKS FOR MAKING ME A BIG SISTER.

Le Cray
BLACK
INTRODUCTION
Samantha!!
me

THIS IS JACOB.
YOU'RE PROBABLY THINKING, "AW, WHAT A CUTE LITTLE GUY!"
TINY, BOUNCY, RED CURLS LIKE A CORKSCREW...
...AND A NOSE AS ROUND AND SMALL AS A BUTTON.

THIS IS ME. MY NAME IS SAMANTHA.
NOW YOU'RE PROBABLY THINKING, "WOW, TWO CUTE, SWEET LITTLE KIDS!"

BUT I KNOW THE TRUTH ABOUT JACOB...

BECAUSE I LIVE WITH HIM.
HE
HE
HE
GET BACK HERE!!
MY BROTHER JACOB IS SOMETHING OF A LEGEND IN MY FAMILY.
AND I HAVE A MILLION TALES I COULD TELL ABOUT HIM.
*NATED ATTAT!
*TRANSLATION: NAKED ATTACK!

EEEH!!! GET OFF OF ME!!
GOTCHA!!
SOME TALES ARE FUNNY...
OTHERS, NOT SO MUCH.
*LEMME DO!!
*LET ME GO!!

GGGGRRRRRRRR...
ONE THING'S FOR SURE...
YEAH, YEAH, BACK IN THE TUB.
...LIFE WITH JACOB IS NEVER BORING.
BUT HE WASN'T ALWAYS THIS "NOT-BORING"...
SIGH

CHAPTER ONE

IN WHICH JACOB EARNS HIS MANY NICKNAMES

ONCE UPON A TIME, JACOB WAS A QUIET, BORING BABY.
WANNA HOLD HIM?
AND I THOUGHT HE WAS PERFECT.

HE NEVER CRIED AND SLEPT ALL DAY, LIKE A CAT.
MOM SLEPT ALL DAY, TOO.
OUR LITTLE APARTMENT WAS VERY QUIET.
MOM SAID SHE HAD THE "BABY BLUES" THAT FIRST MONTH.
MAMA, WAKE UP.
THAT'S HOW I LEARNED THAT "BLUE" MUST MEAN "SAD."
JACOB'S HUNGRY.
BECAUSE SHE WAS SAD ALL THE TIME.

PEEK-A-BOO!
EVENTUALLY, HER SAD "BLUE" TURNED BACK TO HAPPY "YELLOW."
JUST IN TIME FOR ME TO START SCHOOL.
SCHWIP!
GULP

SCHOOL ENDED UP BEING MY FAVORITE THING!
OKAY CLASS, LET'S SING A COUNTING SONG!
READY?!
FIVE GREEN AND SPECKLED FROGS...
SAT ON A SPECKLED LOG! EATING SOME MOST DE...
...LICIOUS BUGS, YUM! YUM!
YEP, LIFE WAS JUST ABOUT PERFECT THEN.

IT ALL STARTED WHEN JACOB LEARNED TO CRAWL.
GOT ANY TENS, MOM?
NOPE, GO FISH!
DARNIT.

I CAN'T REACH!
IT'S MOVING?
WAIT A SEC...
AH! HE'S PUSHING ME!
WOAH, MUSCLES!
LOOK AT 'EM GO!

HE'S TRYING TO GET YOUR ATTENTION!
FEEL LEFT OUT? COME 'ERE, BABY.
HE'S SO STRONG!
DID YOU SEE HOW FAR HE GOT?!
I'VE NEVER SEEN A BABY DO THAT!
HE'S LIKE A-A LIL' HERCULES BABY OR SOMETHING!
THAT'S NOT EASY ON CARPET!! I THINK WE'VE GOT A FUTURE COLLEGE LINEBACKER ON OUR HANDS!
LIL' HERCULES WAS NICKNAME NUMBER ONE.

HIS NEXT NICKNAME WAS "BABY HOUDINI."
ACK! YOUR CARROTS!
THE CARPET!
JACOB?!
...BECAUSE HE WAS AN ESCAPE ARTIST.
BABY HOUDINI COULD SNEAK OUT OF ANYTHING AT ANY TIME...LIKE MAGIC.
UGM

LA DA HMM
FFPT!
A... DIAPER?
JACOB!
WHEW! THERE YOU ARE, YOU BABY HOUDINI.
BA DA DABBA DA!

JACOB WAS SO GOOD AT ESCAPING HIS DIAPER, MOM GOT DESPERATE.
OKAY, HOLD STILL...
SSSCCHH!
SCCRCH!
HEH!
HE TOOK HIS FIRST STEPS IN A DIAPER WRAPPED IN DUCT TAPE.
TAKING CARE OF BABY HOUDINI REQUIRED SOME CREATIVITY.

WANT ME TO READ A BOOK?
JACOB'S THIRD NICKNAME WAS MY SECRET.
NO!!!
MOM! JACOB SAID A WORD!
OKAY, NOW TRY SAYING MY NAME.
CAN YOU SAY SA-MAN-THA?
DUM-DA!
WHAT? NO, MY NAME ISN'T DUMB, IT'S SA-
DUM DUM DUM!!

OKAY! I'M READY!
WHAT WORD WAS IT?
COME BACK AND TALK
FOR THE CAMERA!
DUM DUM DUM
DUM DUM DUM
DUM DUM DUM
DUM DUM DUUUM!
JACOB, DON'T THROW!
WHERE ON EARTH DID
HE LEARN "DUMB"?
THE DUMMY CAN'T SAY
MY NAME RIGHT!

I FELT KINDA BAD FOR CALLING HIM A DUMMY, BUT HE COULDN'T SAY **ANYTHING** RIGHT.
JACOB!! WHAT DO YOU THINK YOU'RE DOING??!!
*IDANT ED TO DWAA DOTZIWA ON TA DOE!
YOU AREN'T ALLOWED TO DRAW ON THE WALLS!!
*I WANTED TO DRAW GODZILLA ON THE DOOR!
*BUDDIT TOOD SKAW OFTA BATDYES!!
*WOAW! EEEETEMUP! GWAR! TOMP! MM!
SAMANTHA, YOU CAN UNDER-STAND HIM...?
*BUT IT WOULD SCARE OFF THE BAD GUYS!!
*ROAR! EAT 'EM UP! RAWR! CHOMP! MMM!

WHEN JACOB WAS FOUR, HE GOT HIS FAMOUS NICKNAME.
MOM, I'M WORRIED HIS BEHAVIOR HAS GOTTEN WORSE...
YESTERDAY HE RAN OUT IN FRONT OF A CAR!
HE JUST BOLTED INTO THE STREET AS FAST AS HE COULD!
I BARELY HAD TIME TO CATCH HIM.
IT DOESN'T SEEM...
...NORMAL.

WHAT IF I HADN'T CAUGHT HIM IN TIME? I'M AFRAID HE'S GONNA HURT HIMSELF EVENTUALLY.
GET AWAY FROM ME!!!
I'M TRYING TO WATCH JURASSIC PARK!

IT'S LIKE LIVING WITH A...TORNADO.

THAT DAY, A LEGEND WAS BORN.
GET BACK HERE YOU... TINY TORNADO!
HAHA!
THE TINY TORNADO
GRANDMA EVEN MADE HIM A SPECIAL T-SHIRT.
JACOB!!
I DIDN'T FIND IT VERY FUNNY.

Le Cray
BLACK
CHAPTER TWO
IN WHICH THE DOCTORS DETERMINE WHETHER JACOB IS A WEIRDO
defntly a weirdo
spot

MOM!! CAN WE GO TO THE PARK?!
FASTER!

!
LALALALALALAAAAA!
WHERE'D JACOB GO?
WWWAAAAAHHHHH!!!!
IS THAT YOUR KID??
YES, SORR-
MICHAEL IS ONLY SIX AND YOUR BIG-BULLY KID PUSHED HIM OFF!

I KNOW HE LOOKS BIG...
...BUT, HE'S ONLY FOUR.
W-WELL. IT WAS MEAN...
SCHOOL WON'T PUT UP WITH THAT BEHAVIOR!
WHAT AM I GONNA DO WITH YOU, KID?
THE ANSWER TO THAT QUESTION WAS A TRIP TO A SPECIAL DOCTOR IN THE CITY.

KANSAS CITY
NEXT 6 EXITS
EXIT ONLY

MAIN ST.

IS JACOB GONNA HAVE TO GET A SURGERY?
*WUT ZA ZEW-GEWY, DUMDA?
*WHAT'S A SURGERY, SAMANTHA?
IT'S WHEN A DOCTOR CUTS YOU OPEN AND TAKES ALL YOUR GUTS AND ORGANS OUT!
THAT'S NOT EVEN TRUE! STOP SCARING YOUR BROTHER!
HEY!!

EVERYTHING IS GOING TO BE JUST FINE!
CHILDREN'S HOSPITAL
EST. 1923
ENTRANCE

WELCOME
WHOA...
EVANS FAMILY?

CHILDREN'S HOSPITAL

THANK YOU.
WAAH!
THE DOCTOR WILL BE IN MOMENTARILY!
BE QUIET FOR ONCE!
HMPH!
OOWW!!
CRUNCH

JACOB!!!
SPIT IT OUT RIG
CDC
WE'RE SORRY!!

OKAY, NOW THAT WE'RE ALL SETTLED DOWN...
YOU'LL SEE HERE THAT THE FLAP OF SKIN UNDER JACOB'S TONGUE IS TOO FAR FORWARD.

HE CAN'T MOVE IT UP AND DOWN AND IT'S CAUSING SPEECH ISSUES.

SO THAT'S IT? A SMALL SURGERY, AND HE'LL BE FINE?

...NOT QUITE. THERE ARE SOME BEHAVIOR ISSUES WE NEED TO TEST, TOO.

UNWRAP IT FIRST!

SO I'M GOING TO SEND YOU HOME WITH INFO ABOUT ADHD AND AUTISM.
AT JACOB'S AGE, IT CAN BE HARD TO TELL THE DIFFERENCE, THOUGH I THINK ADHD IS MORE LIKELY.
WHEN CAN WE FIND OUT FOR SURE?
USUALLY AROUND 5 OR 6 YEARS OLD.
EITHER WAY, JACOB IS GETTING ALL THE CARE HE NEEDS. HE'S HEALTHY AND HAPPY, HE JUST MIGHT NEED SOME EXTRA HELP TO KEEP UP.
BE SURE TO STOP BY SCHEDULING TO MAKE THE SURGERY APPOINTMENT AND A BEHAVIORAL FOLLOW-UP IN 6 MONTHS.

SNORT
ZZZZZ
Z
Z
Z
Z

UGH, READ THIS: "ACTS AS THOUGH DRIVEN BY A MOTOR. ACTS WITHOUT THINKING."
SOUNDS LIKE THE TINY TORNADO TO ME...
HERE IT SAYS, "BECOMES EASILY FRUSTRATED, HAS TROUBLE WORKING WITH OTHERS."
ADHD STANDS FOR: "ATTENTION DEFICIT HYPER-ACTIVITY DISORDER."
WELL, HE'S "HYPER" ALRIGHT...

WOW, MOM AND DAD ARE PRETTY WORRIED ABOUT JACOB...
...MAYBE I'VE BEEN TOO MEAN TO HIM LATELY...
AHHHHH!!
WHAT ARE YOU DOING?!
HA HA
YOU BROKE ALL OF THEM.
DOLLS

POP!
*BYE-BYE DUBBIE DAW!
*BYE-BYE BARBIE DOLL!
YOU ARE THE WORS
D I
HAT
U!!!
I HOPE THE DOCTORS STICK SOMETHING IN YOUR BRAIN THAT MAKES YOU NORMAL...

SOB GO AWAY!
ARE WE READY FOR BED YET?
GOOD NIGHT, TINY TORNADO.
YOU WERE SUCH A BIG HELP TODAY.
WE COUNT ON YOU SO MUCH.

GUILT
GUILT
GUILT
CLICK!
JACOB?
ARE YOU ASLEEP?

SORRY...

Le Cray
BLACK
CHAPTER THREE
IN WHICH SAMANTHA MUST LEARN TO BE NICE TO JACOB (BUT HE MAKES IT SO HARD)
Say hi to the Sharks!
Ship to: Pacific Ocean

EVEN THOUGH EVERYONE WAS WORRIED, THINGS STAYED PRETTY MUCH THE SAME.
ROAR GRRRR
Le Crayon
$3.99
GLUE
NOT NOW.
Le Crayon

JACOB GOT THE SURGERY TO FIX HIS TONGUE.
HMPH.
HE COULDN'T TALK FOR A DAY.
HA HA HA
YOU'LL SHOOT YER EYE OUT!!
WE HAD A CALM EVENING FOR ONCE.

JACOB
THE DOCTORS RECOMMENDED JACOB START PRESCHOOL THAT SPRING.
FUN!
Aa Bb Cc Dd Ee F
THEY WANTED TO SEE HOW HE ACTED AWAY FROM HOME.
FIRST DAY WORRIES? WE'LL TAKE GOOD CARE OF HIM.
IT'S NOT REALLY **HIM** I'M WORRIED FOR...
WITHIN 2 WEEKS, HIS TEACHER HAD FILLED OUT THE DOCTOR'S PAPERWORK.
OH, THANKS.
IT WAS LOOKING LIKE JACOB HAD ADHD.

PLEASE SEE DRAWING MADE BY JACOB, VERY CONCERNING.
WHAT ON EARTH IS SHE TALKING–
Very concerned about this... Did Jacob watch something violent recently?
SIGH NO MORE DINOSAUR MOVIES FOR YOU, BUDDY.

HI SAMANTHA! GRANDMA'S INSIDE GETTING SETUP.
MOM'S LITTLE SISTER, MY AUNT LULU, WAS GETTING MARRIED THAT SPRING.
WE CAME OVER TO HELP WITH FLOWERS A FEW DAYS BEFORE.
VIDEO GAMES WERE THE ONLY WAY TO KEEP JACOB OUT OF THE WAY.

I'LL DO THESE ONES!
NO, THIS IS FOR GROWN-UPS. GO PLAY.
HMPH!

A FEW HOURS LATER...
OKAY, ALL DONE. TIME TO GO, GET YOUR COATS.
KO!
HA! I BEAT YOU AGAIN!
WHACK!

*SORRY, SAMANTHA.

BACK AT HOME
GO PLAY IN YOUR ROOM.
HEY, YOU OKAY? DOES YOUR HEAD STILL HURT?
I'M FINE.
WHY IS JACOB SO **HORRIBLE?!**

SAMANTHA, YOU DON'T MEAN THAT. JACOB ISN'T HORRIBLE.
HE SHOULD'NT HAVE HIT YOU LIKE THAT, I'M SORRY...
HE HAS A HARDER TIME CONTROLLING HIS ANGER.
WHY CAN'T HE BE MORE LIKE ME? BE...NORMAL.
YOU KNOW THAT LITTLE VOICE IN YOUR HEAD THAT KEEPS YOU FROM DOING SOMETHING DANGEROUS OR EMBARRASSING?
YOU MEAN, LIKE MY... CONSCIENCE?
NO, MORE LIKE YOUR "CAREFUL" VOICE THAT MAKES YOU PAUSE.

JACOB DOESN'T HAVE A "CAREFUL" VOICE, HE JUST DOES STUFF.
BUT I'M CARE-FUL ABOUT EVERYTHING ALL THE TIME...WHY CAN'T HE BE LIKE ME AND THINK BEFORE HE HURTS ME OR MY TOYS? IT'S NOT FAIR...
EVERYONE'S BRAIN IS DIFFERENT. JACOB HAS TROUBLE CONTROLLING HIS IMPULSES...LIKE, HE DOES STUFF WITHOUT THINKING FIRST. IT DOESN'T MEAN HE'S BAD. HE JUST NEEDS US TO BE HIS "CAREFUL" VOICE FOR A WHILE.

I CAN'T IMAGINE NOT BEING CAREFUL...

THAT'S BECAUSE YOU WORRY TOO MUCH SOMETIMES.

WHAT ABOUT WHEN HE'S HITTING?
YOU COME STRAIGHT TO ME. HITTING IS NOT OKAY.
HE MAKES ME **SO** MAD SOMETIMES I HIT HIM BACK OR SAY MEAN THINGS...
AND THEN I FEEL SO BAD FOR BEING ANGRY.
WE'RE ALL GOING TO HAVE TO LEARN TO BE EXTRA PATIENT.

TABAT A SAT TEDDIOS DI NAW!
HE SAID HE WANTS SPAGHETTIOS.
LUNCHTIME!

FINALLY, IT WAS THE DAY OF THE WEDDING!
SINCE I WAS A FLOWER GIRL, I GOT A NEW DRESS.
I WAS SO EXCITED TO SEE HOW MUCH EVERYONE WOULD LOVE IT.
IS SHE FAMOUS?!
WOW, SO CUTE!
BEST FLOWER GIRL EVER!
IN REALITY, AFTER MY PART, IT WAS PRETTY BORING...
DO YOU

AFTERWARDS, THERE WAS A BIG RECEPTION.
IT WAS THE FANCIEST ROOM I HAD EVER STOOD IN...AND THERE WAS CAKE!

AT THE END
OKED
VELY
HONEYMOO

LET'S GROOVE TO A RETRO BEAT!

*DASS, DUM?
OKAAAY...
*DANCE, SAMANTHA?
DAAAA HOO!!!
DON'T MAKE ME REGRET SAYING YES!
!
ZOOM

EVERYONE IS STARING AT US...

*DASS! DUS DASS!
* DANCE! JUST DANCE!
BUT IT'S...EMBARRASSING...
IF JACOB CAN DO IT...
SO CAN I!!

A FEW HOURS LATER...
WE SHOULD TRY TO GO TO MORE WEDDINGS!

Le Cray
BLACK
CHAPTER FOUR
IN WHICH "BABY HOUDINI" PERFORMS HIS GREATEST STUNT YET
tadah!

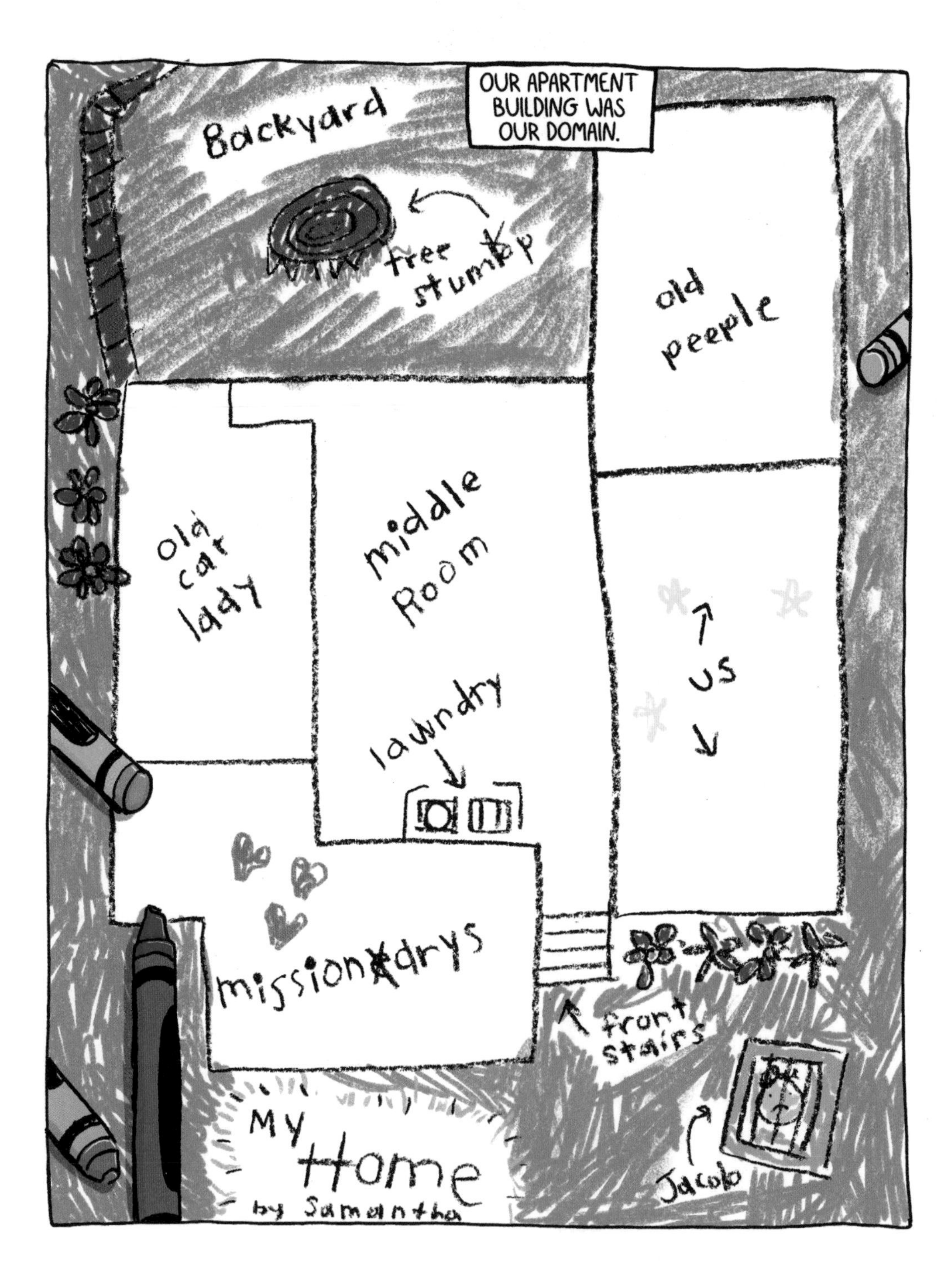
OUR APARTMENT BUILDING WAS OUR DOMAIN.
Backyard
tree stump
old peeple
old cat lady
middle Room
laundry
us
missionarys
front stairs
My Home
by Samantha
Jacob

BEFORE LONG, SUMMER WAS BACK.
WE WERE THE ONLY KIDS WHO LIVED ON OUR ENTIRE STREET.
THIS WAS GOOD AND BAD...
GOOD: WE WERE ADORED.
CHALK
CLEARLY BORED
OH SAMANTHA, YOU'RE SO TALENTED!
CRUNCH!
CHRUNCH!
CRUNCH!
THANK YOU.
HAM
MY CHALK!
CRUNCH!
BAD: I ONLY HAD ONE PLAYMATE.

*THERE'S A BAT IN YOUR HAIR!!

THE ONLY OTHER YOUNG PEOPLE WERE TWO MISSIONARIES.
HI EVANS FAMILY!
*PAWSIKEWS!!
THEY WERE NICE...
*POPSICLES!!
POPSICLE COMING UP!
THINK THAT YOU SHOULD READ
THEY'D GIVE US POPSICLES WHILE THEY TALKED TO MY PARENTS ABOUT BOOKS.
SPIRIT WHEN I READ FROM THE BOOK
I THOUGHT THEY WERE TERRIBLY HANDSOME.
THANKS FOR LISTENING!
OF COURSE!
YEAH, OF COURSE.

THE ONLY THING IN THE ENTIRE BACKYARD WAS AN OLD TREE STUMP IN THE VERY CENTER.
SO, WE HAD TO BE CREATIVE.

SOMETIMES IT WAS A PERFECT TABLE.
FOR TEA...

BBLLLAAAAHH!!!
...OR AN OPERATION.

RED LIGHT!
RED LIGHT!
IT COULD BE A FINISH LINE.
HMPH!
*DIDN!
*I WIN!
AND SOMETIMES A STAGE.
THANK YOU!
WE NEVER WORE SHOES IF WE COULD HELP IT.
AND JACOB NEVER WORE PANTS.

OTHER DAYS, IT WAS TOO HOT TO PLAY OUTSIDE.
SO WE PLAYED OUT IN THE COMMON AREA INSTEAD.
BUT USUALLY, I SPENT MY SUMMERS READING IN BED.
*ATTAT!!
LEAVE ME ALONE!
*ATTACK!!

*OTAY, FIBE.
*OKAY, FINE.
WOW, CAN'T BELIEVE THAT WORKED...
TO mom
A 1
SIGH WHAT A QUIET DAY...
TICK TOCK
TICK TOCK
IT'S TOO QUIET.

JAAAACOB!!
. . .
JACOB!!
JACOB?!
WHERE YA AT?
COME OUT NOW!
WHERE IS HE...?

HAVE YOU SEEN YOUR BROTHER??
NOT FOR A WHILE...
MAYBE HE'S IN THE MIDDLE ROOM.
JACOB...??
JACOB?!!
WHERE ARE YOU?!!

JACOB! ANSWER ME RIGHT NOW!!!
JACOB!!
DO YOU HEAR HIM? HE'S CLOSE!
*DUH DUN A WAB BA GABBO DO SOWAH!!
*NO TRASNLATION FOUND

BUT...WHERE IS HE...?
LOOK!! THERE HE IS IN THE WINDOW!!!
DOOK ATDEE! DU GOBBA DET A PAWSIKAW AN TAWB AH ADO!
ISN'T THAT THE MISSIONARIES' APARTMENT WINDOW?
ZOOM
JACOB!!! HOW ON EARTH DID YOU GET IN THERE??!! GET OUT RIGHT NOW!!

OPE!
OH NO OH NO OH NO O-
HE FREAKIN' LOCKED IT!
1B
1B
OPEN THIS DOOR RIGHT NOW OR ELSE!!! YOU HEAR ME?! YOU ARE GONNA BE IN SO MUCH TROUBLE!!!
BUMP!
I CAN HEAR HIM RUNNING!

1B
YOU HAVE UNTIL I COUNT TO THREE! ONE! TWO! THR-
CLICK!
OH THANK GOODNESS!!!
1B
...JACOB?

GASP THE POPSICLES!
AHH!
POP!
HE MICROWAVED HIS FAVORITE HOT WHEELS...?
THUMP!
YOU ARE IN SO MUCH TROUBLE, MISTER!

WHAT DO YOU THINK YOU'RE DOING??!!
*TUMPIND.
*JUMPING.
WAAH WAAAA NO!!!
...AND WE WILL REPLACE THE MICROWAVE AND POPSICLES...
1 HOUR LATER...
*PAWSICKWES?!
*POPSICLES?!
HAHAHA, THAT'S HILARIOUS!
WE SHOULD PROBABLY LOCK OUR DOOR, HA.

* I WANT MY RACE CAR BACK.

Le Cray
BLACK
CHAPTER FIVE
IN WHICH JACOB-ZILLA TRIES TO RUIN MY LIFE
NO!!

BEFORE LONG, SCHOOL STARTED BACK UP.
NEW BACKPACK!
MOM WOULD DRIVE JACOB SO I COULD RIDE THE BUS ALONE.
FIRST-AID
SCHOOL WAS MY HAPPY PLACE: READING TIME, RECESS, AND ART CLASS! AND ALL WITHOUT SOMEONE JUMPING ON ME OR SCREAMING.

ALSO, MY BIRTHDAY WAS NEAR THE START OF SCHOOL.
APPY BIRTHDAY TOOO YOOOUUU! HAPPY BIRTHDAY TOOOO YOOOUUU!
DEAR SA-MANTHAA!
HAAA!
HEEEY!
*DODZIWA!
*GODZILLA!
JACOB WAS SENT TO HIS ROOM FOR THE REST OF THE PARTY.
A...BOWL?
FISH

SAMANTHA!
GASP!
A FISHY!!!
GOLDIE WAS MY VERY FIRST PET.
SHE WAS PERFECT IN EVERY WAY.
I COULD WATCH HER FLOAT IN HER BOWL FOR HOURS...
*SHISHY!
SHE DIDN'T STAND A CHANCE...

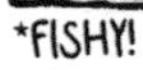
*FISHY!

THAT FALL, MOM DEEP CLEANED THE CARPET.
300 POWER STEAM.O
SHE RENTED A BIG VACUUM.
SSSSSSS
EVERYTHING WAS PILED UP AROUND THE PLACE.
AND THE STEAM OF THE VACUUM MADE THE CARPET HOT.
THE FLOOR IS LAVA!!
IT MADE OUR DEADLY OBSTACLE COURSE FEEL EXTRA REALISTIC.

HEY!
HMPH!
YOU RUIN EVERYTHING FUN!
WOOOAR!
CRASH

JACOB!!! NOT THE FISH!!
AAAAAARRRHHH!!!

SHE'S BLEEDING!
STAY BACK FROM THE GLASS!
MOM! HURRY! SAVE GOLDIE!!!
SHE CAN'T BREATHE!!
SHE'LL DIE!!
JACOB IS HURT TOO, SAMANTHA!
FLIP
FLOP
TWITCH
TWITCH

SOB MOM, PLEASE!! *SOB*
GIVE ME 10 SECONDS!!
I PROMISE!
ONE...TWO...
THREE...FOUR...
FIVE...SIX...
SEVEN...EIGHT...
...NINE...

...TEN!
DON'T HURT HER!!
IS SHE GONNA BE OKAAAAY...?
I DON'T KNOW.
PLUNK!

GOLDIE...?

WAAAAH!!

I NEED TO CHECK ON JACOB.

SURE!! SEE IF THE MURDERER IS OK!

WELL I DON'T CARE IF JACOB'S OKAY!!

I WAS TOO UPSET TO LEAVE MY ROOM.
PAT
NOT FOR DAD OR EVEN TO EAT DINNER.
MY POOR GOLDIE...
Z Z
*SHISHY DIVE!

*FISHY DIED!

GO. AWAY.
SHISHY DIVE!!!
I SAID GO!
SHI-SHY DIIIVE!
YEP! "SHISHY" DIED ALRIGHT, AND IT'S YOUR FAULT!!

LOOK WHAT YOU DID.
SHISHY DIVE!

SHISHY DIVE! SHSIHY DIVE!

GOLDIE!!
"SHISHY DIVE" MEANS "FISHY ALIVE," HAHA!

MOM!!
SHSIHY DIVE!!!

THE REST OF THE YEAR WENT BY QUICKLY AND QUIETLY.
UNTIL...
WE HAVE SOME BIG NEWS...
*GAW-ZIWA?!!!
*GODZILLA?!!!
NO, WE'RE HAVING ANOTHER BABY!
AND WE'RE MOVING!
*BABEE GAW-ZIWA!
WHY?!
*BABY GODZILLA!
WE'RE NOT MOVING VERY FAR AWAY...
UUGGGGGGH
...AND YOU'LL GET YOUR OWN ROOM.
HM?

MY OWN ROOM?
MY OWN ROOM...
I'LL START PACKING!!

MOVING DAY!!!

HURRY UP
HURRY UP!!

IT'S
HUGE!

LET'S SCOPE THE
PLACE OUT.

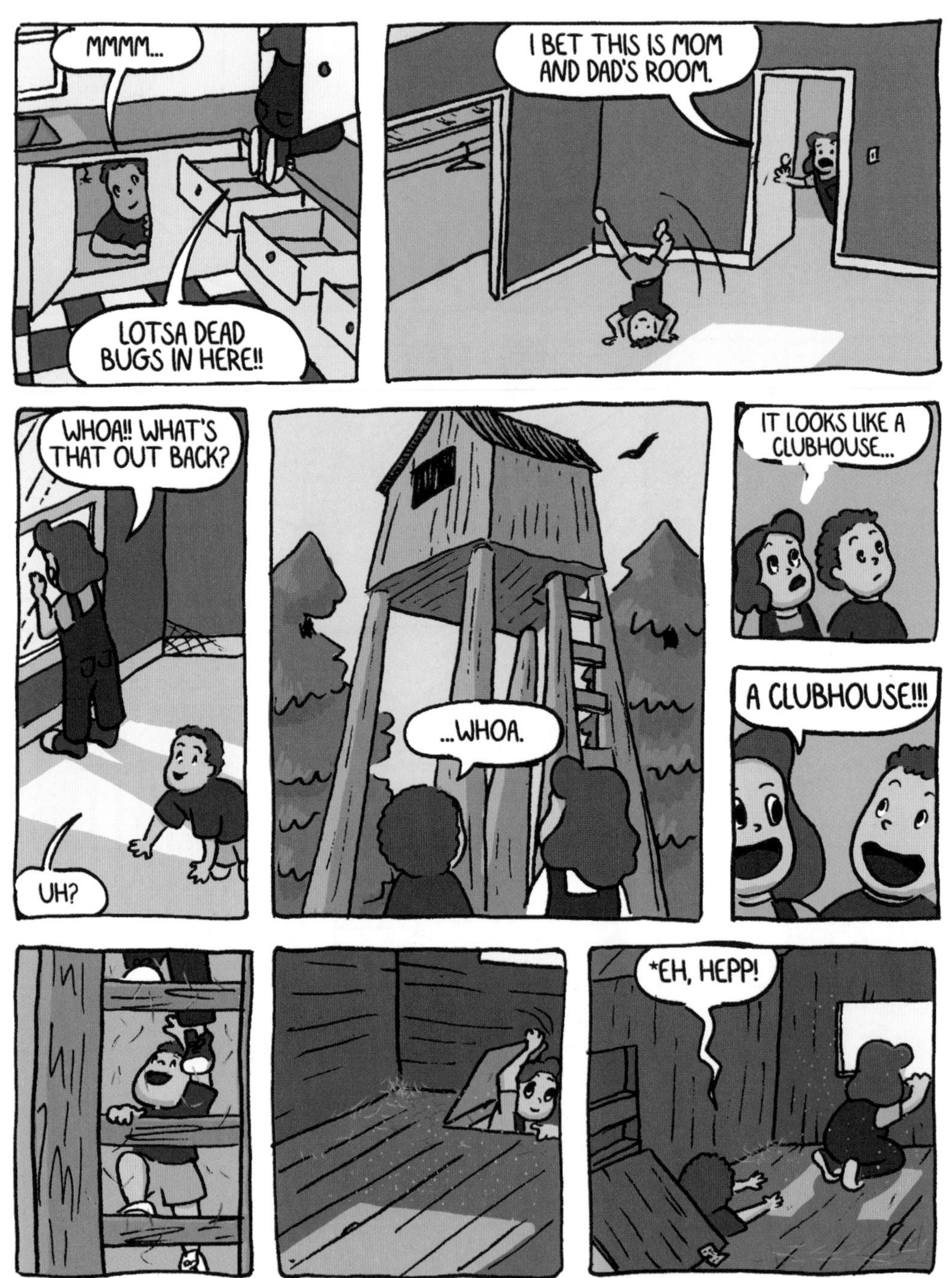
MMMM...
LOTSA DEAD BUGS IN HERE!!
I BET THIS IS MOM AND DAD'S ROOM.
WHOA!! WHAT'S THAT OUT BACK?
UH?
...WHOA.
IT LOOKS LIKE A CLUBHOUSE...
A CLUBHOUSE!!!
*EH, HEPP!

*AH, HELP!

I CAN SEE EVERYTHING!
WOOOOW!
LET'S GO BACK IN.
WHICH ROOM IS MINE???
FIRST DOOR ON THE LEFT!
Samantha's Room
Samantha's Room

I SPENT THE REST OF THE DAY UNPACKING.
ALL MY STUFF LOOKED THE SAME...
SPACE
SPACE
SPACE
...JUST MORE SPREAD OUT AND SAD.
CAN WE GO TO TARGET FOR ROOM DECORATIONS?
HA! WHEN ON EARTH HAVE WE **EVER** GONE TO TARGET?

THAT NIGHT WE GOT PIZZA AND ATE OUTSIDE.
*GOTSUN!
*CAUGHT ONE!
AW, SO CUTE!
SPLAT!
MOM!!

EVENTUALLY I GOT SOME HAND-ME-DOWN FURNITURE.
AND AN ART DESK!!
FRIDA
MY ROOM WAS MY SANCTUARY FROM THE CHAOS OF JACOB.

MY OTHER FAVORITE PLACE WAS THE APPLE TREE IN THE BACKYARD. I WAS A GOOD CLIMBER...
...AND JACOB WAS NOT.

Le Cray
BLACK
CHAPTER SIX
IN WHICH JACOB DEFEATS THE NEIGHBORHOOD BULLIES
roar!!
yay!

OUR NEW STREET ACTUALLY HAD OTHER KIDS TO PLAY WITH!
*BING MITEW!
MOM!! JACOB IS FOLLOWING ME!!
*BRING ME TOO!
TAKE HIM WITH YOU!
UHHHH! ARE YOU KIDDING ME?!!! FIIINE!
YOU BETTER KEEP UP!
SLOW DOWN!!

THERE WERE THREE 6TH GRADE BOYS WHO HUNG OUT AT THE END OF MY STREET. THEY INVITED ME ALONG, TOO.
GAVIN
BRANDON
ALEX
GAME BUY
HEY, NEW GIRL!
WAIT UP, GUYS!
DEAD END
YOU BROUGHT YOUR FREAKY BROTHER!
*I DONNA PEED AN DA TWEEE.
DEAD END
*I'M GONNA PEE ON A TREE.
HEH HEH. YEAH, MY MOM MADE ME...
I SAW HIM EAT PRE-CHEWED GUM ON THE BUS YESTERDAY.
I BET THIS LIL' FREAK WILL DO ANYTHING YOU ASK HIM TO.
UHHH, I GUESS...
HERE, BITE MY SKATEBOARD, HAHA!
CHOMP!

C'MON, WE'RE GONNA BREAK BOTTLES IN THE WOODS!
SOUNDS FUN!
*DESTWUCKSON!
*DESTRUCTION!
DID YOU HEAR ABOUT THE KIDS WHO GOT MURDERED IN THESE WOODS?
KEEP UP, FREAKS!
IT'S NOT TRUE, THEY'RE JUST TRYING TO SCARE US, OKAY?

SMASH!
HAHA, NICE ONE GAVIN!!

WHOAA! DOPE, DUDE!
*I BOWD.
BE COOL...
*I'M BORED.
WHAT ARE THEY DOING...?
HEY, THEY'RE CLIMBING TREES, I CAN DO THAT! COME ON!
GUYS, BOOST ME UP!!

NO FREAKS ALLOWED!!
THESE GUYS STINK, LET'S GET OUT OF HERE...
*EY NOTTA FEEK EW-AR!!
*I'M NOT A FREAK, YOU ARE!!
HAHAHAHA, CAN YOU UNDERSTAND HIM???
I MISSED ON PURPOSE! DON'T TRY ME, FREAK!

YOU GUYS ARE JERKS!!
AHHH!
COME ON, LET'S GO!

AAAAAAAAAAAHHHHHHHHHHHH
OMPH!

OH MY GOD,
ARE YOU
DEAD???
ROOAAR!!
LET'S GET OUT
OF HERE!!
I'M SORRY!!

ARE YOU OKAY??
*I SOWWY I TAD DO FENDS A WAY...
*I'M SORRY I SCARED YOUR FRIENDS AWAY...
ARE YOU KIDDING?? THOSE GUYS WERE JERKS! THAT WAS THE COOLEST THING EVER!
BUT LET'S NOT TELL MOM, OKAY?
*OTAY, DUM.
*OKAY, SAMANTHA.

FALL ROLLED IN, AND WITH IT CAME LOTS OF CHANGES...
AHHH! DOOON'T!!!
SOME OF THE CHANGES WERE GOOD, OTHERS WERE... WORRISOME.

ONE GOOD CHANGE...
SINCE YOU'VE DONE SUCH A GOOD JOB WITH GOLDIE...
...WAS A NEW FAMILY MEMBER.
...WE THINK YOU CAN HANDLE A LITTLE MORE RESPONSIBILITY.
YOU CAN OPEN YOUR EYES.
WHAT WILL YOU NAME HER?

LUCY!!
THE WORRISOME CHANGE THAT WAS COMING...
...WAS ALSO A NEW FAMILY MEMBER.
I GOT IT, MOM! YOU CAN SIT DOWN!
HEY, I CAN FEEL THE BABY KICKING! HAHA, WOW!

...WOW, THEY'RE KICKING
REALLY, REALLY HARD...
PLEASE DON'T BE LIKE JACOB.
PLEASE DON'T BE LIKE JACOB.
AND THEN ONE DAY, JUST LIKE THAT, BABY WAS THERE FASTER THAN A BLINK.
GRANDMA, WHAT ARE YOU DOING HERE...?
YOUR MOM JUST HAD THE BABY A FEW HOURS AGO!
WE'LL VISIT HER AFTER DINNER.

BABY LUKE WAS VERY DIFFERENT THAN JACOB.
MOM DIDN'T GET THE "BABY BLUES" LIKE LAST TIME.
BABY LUKE WAS ALSO MUCH SMALLER THAN JACOB WAS AS A BABY.
BABY LUKE SIZE
BABY JACOB SIZE
HOPEFULLY, HE WOULD BE A MUCH CALMER LITTLE BROTHER.
A PERFECT LITTLE THING.

JACOB WAS UNSURE ABOUT THE BABY.
WOULD YOU LIKE TO HOLD YOUR NEW LITTLE BROTHER, LUKE?
NOOOOO!!

HE DIDN'T QUITE UNDERSTAND THE POINT OF HAVING A BABY AROUND.
THEY DIDN'T TASTE PARTICULARLY GOOD.
NO FANGS, EITHER.
AND APPARENTLY, NEW BABIES COULDN'T PLAY WITH TOYS **AT ALL**.

BUT THEN...
HHHMMMNN!!
...LUKE DID SOMETHING.
PPFT!
THBT!
WHEW! SOMEBODY NEEDS A DIAPER CHANGE!
*TINK-EE DUKE.
AND HE DECIDED BABIES WERE AWESOME.

*STINKY LUKE.

Le Cray
BLACK
CHAPTER SEVEN
IN WHICH NO ANIMALS WERE HARMED IN THE MAKING OF THIS CHAPTER, (JUST MADE VERY ANGRY...)
Bzz
Hiss!

THE REST OF THE YEAR MARCHED ON.
202

AND BEFORE WE KNEW IT...

...IT WAS SUMMER AGAIN.
AND WE WERE DETERMINED TO TAME OUR CLUBHOUSE.
D.I.R.E
D.I.R.E

*WHAT THE HECK?!!

GASP SORRY!
*WUT HAPPAND?
*WHAT HAPPENED?
THERE'S A HUGE WASP NEST UP THERE!
BZZ
BZZZ ZZZ
BZZZ
WELL! WHAT ARE WE SUPPOSED TO DO NOW?!
WE GOTTA GET THOSE WASPS OUTTA THERE.

ACK, IT'S DARK! WHERE'S THE STRING THINGY??
CLICK!
DIRE
OKAY, LOOK FOR BUG SPRAY!
OPE! OVER HERE!!
THIS LOOKS DEADLY!
"FOR BLACK WIDOWS, BROWN RECLUSE, AND OTHER..."
SPIDERS
OH, I THINK THIS IS JUST FOR SPIDERS.

*WUD IT TIW WOWK?
*WOULD IT STILL WORK?
NAW, DAD WOULD BE MAD IF WE USED IT WRONG.
I DON'T KNOW WHAT TO DO...
*WUT-TA BOT WUCEY?
*WHAT ABOUT LUCY?
YES, GENIUS! SHE'S THE BEST BUG-HUNTER IN THE WORLD! I BET SHE'D DESTROY THOSE WASPS!!
D.I.R.E.
COME ON! I BET I KNOW WHERE SHE IS!

*LUCY'S GONNA GET THOSE WASPS.

LET'S GO, MY LITTLE BUG WARRIOR!
D.I.R.E.
OKAY, HOLD HER WHILE I CLIMB UP, THEN HAND HER TO ME WHEN I SAY!
D.I.R.E.
OKAY, HAND HER UP TO ME!! DON'T DROP HER!

HURRY! GET BACK BEFORE THE FIGHTING STARTS!
CAN YOU SEE ANYTHING?
IS SHE EATING THE WASPS?
NOTHING'S HAPPENING!
WHAT IS SHE EVEN DOING UP THERE? COME ON, CAT!
D.I.R.E

OKAY, WE NEED A NEW PLAN...
THERE HAS TO BE SOMETHING.
D.I.R.E
GOT ANYTHING?
*NUP.
*NOPE.
THINK, SAMANTHA, THINK...
SWINGS...? SLIDE...? NOPE.

THROW APPLES?
HMM, NO...
I BET THERE'S SOMETHING WE COULD USE IN THE SHED, BUT IT'S LOCKED...
BINGO!

THE WATER HOSE!
WE'LL BLAST THAT WASP NEST TO SMITHEREENS!! HEH HEH HEH!
OKAY, IN POSITION?!
*DEP!
*YEP!
WHEN I SAY "NOW," TURN IT ON. WE SHOULD HAVE A FEW MINUTES BEFORE MOM NOTICES!
BZZZ

READY!
CCCHHHSSSHA

SMASH!
AAH! IT WORKED!
*ID WEWKED!
*IT WORKED!
SEE, ALL THE WASPS FLEW AWAY!!

*LOOK, THERE'S LUCY!

WHOOPS...

QUICK, GRAB HER!
ZOOOOMM
NO LUCY, COME 'ERE. HERE, KITTY!

LUCY, I'M SORRY!
MRRRRRR...
LUCY HID UNDER THE PORCH FOR THREE DAYS.
I'M SORRY, PLEASE COME OUT...
HHHSSSK!
BUT AT LEAST WE GOT THE WASPS TO LEAVE!

I WORKED SO HARD ON THE CLUBHOUSE AND MADE IT ABSOLUTELY PERFECT!
I PUT UP SOME DECORATIONS...
A BOOKSHELF,
A SECURITY SYSTEM,
EVEN A WEATHER MONITOR!
IT WAS MY NEW QUIET, HAPPY PLACE WHERE I COULD BE ALONE...

*HEY MANTA! I GONNA TUM UP!
*DET ME IN!
I DEFINITELY DIDN'T WANT MY QUIET PLACE RUINED...
*HEY SAMANTHA, I'M GONNA COME UP!
*LET ME IN!
HMP!
WHOA!
FINE!!
I FELT A LITTLE BAD ABOUT THAT...

Le Cray
BLACK
CHAPTER EIGHT
IN WHICH JACOB DEALS WITH SOME SCHOOL STUFF
2 COOL 4 School

BEFORE WE KNEW IT, SCHOOL WAS STARTING BACK UP...
THIS YEAR, I'D BE RIDING THE BIG KID BUS.
SMILE!
OKAY, JUST A FEW MORE!!
I'M GONNA MISS THE BUS!
OKAY, SAMANTHA.
SAY CHEESE!
FINALLY, BACK TO SCHOOL...

HMMM...
I WONDER WHAT SCHOOL IS LIKE FOR JACOB?
DOES HE LIKE IT AS MUCH AS I DO?
Mr. Conner
Mrs. Jenkins
SOCCER

HI JACOB, MY NAME IS MISS BRYAN.
IT'S NICE TO MEET YOU! ARE YOU EXCITED FOR 2ND GRADE?
HEAD ON IN, AND PICK A SEAT!
*WACH DIS!
WHACK
TAH DUH!!
*WATCH THIS!
FROM NOW ON, LET'S TAKE OUR BACKPACK OFF THE NORMAL WAY...
*WHATS A NOMAW WAY?
*WHAT'S A NORMAL WAY?

HELLO EVERYONE AND WELCOME TO 2ND GRADE! I AM SO EXCITED TO BE YOUR TEACHER THIS YEAR. TODAY WE'RE GOING TO FOCUS ON
1 MINUTE INTO SCHOOL...
4 MINUTES INTO SCHOOL...
JACOB!
WHACK!
5 MINUTES INTO SCHOOL...
JACOB, PLEASE STAND UP STRAIGHT!
1...2...3...4...5!
IT'S MY TURN.
DDFFT!

WWWAAAHHH!
BE KIND!
JACOB, ROTATIONS ARE OVER!
SHARE, JACOB!
JACOB! NO PUSHING!
JACOB, CAN YOU TRY AGAIN, USING THE DIFFERENT COLORS WE LEARNED?
EWWWW! GROSS!
LEAVE THE CLASS PET ALONE!!

JACOB, I KNOW IT'S HARD, BUT I NEED YOU TO SIT STILL...
...AND BE CALM SO YOU DON'T DISTURB THE REST OF THE CLASS.
THINK YOU CAN DO THAT, BUD?
YEAH!
OKAY, HEAD ON IN, AND BE MY LEADER ON THE READING RUG.
OKAY CLASS, IT'S STORYTIME!
JOIN ME ON THE READING RUG!

NO, DAVID!
OH BOY! CLASS, WHAT IS DAVID
DOING IN THIS
*YOU TAN DO DIS, DUST...
*YOU CAN DO THIS, JUST...
"HOLD STILL"
"BE CALM"
DON'T YELL...

"SETTLE DO-"
*SETTEW DOWN DABID! OR YOUW DIE!
*SETTLE DOWN DAVID! OR YOU'LL DIE!
SIGH
WAAAAH HA HA HA HA!!
JACOB! GO FLIP YOUR CITIZENSHIP STICK TO RED. THAT IS UNACCEPTABLE!
YOU'LL HAVE TO SIT ON THE SIDELINE AT RECESS!
JACOB?! HOW WAS SCHOOL?

LATER THAT DAY...
JACOB?
IS YOUR TEACHER NICE? MAKE ANY FRIENDS?
*I DON WANNA TAWK ABOUT IT.
*I DON'T WANNA TALK ABOUT IT.
OKAY, I WAS JUST-
*NO! WEAVE ME AWONE!
*NO! LEAVE ME ALONE!
Jacob
Jacob
WHACK!

NO DOOR SLAMMING!!
YOU'LL HURT SOME-ONE DOING THAT! YOU HEAR ME?
JACOB...?
JACO
WHAM!!
HEY!!
I THINK HE HAD A REALLY BAD FIRST DAY OF SCHOOL.
SIGH OKAY, I'LL TALK TO HIM.

JACOB'S BAD MOOD LASTED ALL WEEK. HE'D STOMP OFF THE BUS,
THEN SIT ON THE COUCH AND POUT WITHOUT MOVING.
IT WAS WEIRD TO SEE HIM SO QUIET.
I'D TRY TO CHEER HIM UP WITH HIS FAVORITE THINGS, BUT IT DIDN'T WORK.
HEY, LET'S PLAY SMASH BROTHERS!
*WEAVE ME A AWONE!
*LEAVE ME ALONE!

THAT WEEKEND,
I DECIDED TO GET HIM TO PLAY OUTSIDE WITH ME AND GET SOME EXERCISE, HOPING IT WOULD HELP.
OKAY, I'M GONNA SHOW YOU HOW TO PLAY WIFFLE BALL!
THIS IS THE WIFFLE BALL, YOU'LL KNOW BECAUSE IT'S FULL OF HOLES!
IT'S A LOT LIKE BASEBALL, 'CEPT WE DON'T HAVE REAL BASES.

THAT SHOE IS FIRST BASE,
THE APPLES ARE SECOND,
AND A PAINT CAN FOR THIRD!
THAT HOOP IS HOME BASE AND WHERE YOU'LL BAT!
DO YOU WANT TO PLAY?!
YEAH!
OKAY, YOU BAT FIRST!
HEHE.
EASY...

READY??!!
YEAH!

*EY MIST!!
*I MISSED!!
IT'S OKAY, TRY AGAIN!!!
GRRMMMRBBMLLL
*I TANT DO ANYTING WIGHT...
*I CAN'T DO ANYTHING RIGHT...
UMPH!
WHAT THE HECK?! WHY'D YOU DO THAT???

*I'M SORRY, SAMANTHA.

*SOWY MANTA...
*SORRY SAMANTHA...
HEH!

*WHERE'S THAT BALL...?

*BINGO!

RUFF! RUFF!
RUFFF RUF RUFF!
WOOF! WOOF!
*DODS!!!
*DOGS!!!
RUUUFF RUFFRUFF!
WOOF! WOOOF OOF! WOOF!!
AAAAAAAAAHHHHHHHHHHCCCCCCHHH!
PANT
SSLP!

SIGH THANKS A LOT, JACOB...
KNOCK
KNOCK
WHAT?
HI MISS BEACHES, I'M YOUR NEIGHBOR, SAMANTHA, AND I WAS WONDERIN-
AAHHHHCCCCHH!!..
WAS THAT...JACOB SCREAMING...?
WHAT'S THAT RACKET?!

HHHEEEWWWPPP!!!
JACOB!!
I'M COMING!!
JACOB?!!
WHERE IS HE?
I SWEAR I HEARD HIM...

HHHEEEWWWPPP!!!
HE'S IN MISS BEACHES' YARD?!
*HEWP!! HEWP!! HEWP!!
*HELP!! HELP!! HELP!!
I'M ON MY WAY, JACOB!!
HHEEH!

I'LL SAVE YOU!! I'LL-
AHHHH!
...SAVE YOU?
THEY'RE NOT ATTACKING AT ALL...
JACOB, LET GO!!
YOU'RE *HHUUH* SQUEEZING THEM!

HEWP! HEWP HEEEEWP! WAAAH HAH HAH AAAH
HE'S GOING TO STRANGLE MY DOGS!!
JACOB, LET GO!
THEY WON'T HURT YOU, THEY'RE FRIENDLY DOGS.
OH!

*DOD FWENDS!
*DOG FRIENDS!
HERE'S YOUR BALL, GET OUT OF MY YARD!
BYE, DOGGIES!
HMNK!
AAH HAHA HA!!
WUT?!
YOU LIVE UP TO YOUR "LIL' HERCULES" NICKNAME!
*WUT IS DAT SUPPOWSED TO MENE?
*WHAT IS THAT SUPPOSED TO MEAN?

HERCULES
SEE, THIS IS THE DEMIGOD HERCULES AS A BABY.
HE WAS SO STRONG THAT HE STRANGLED TWO SNAKES THAT SNUCK INTO HIS CRIB!
WE USED TO CALL YOU "LIL' HERCULES" BECAUSE YOU WERE SO STRONG AS A BABY.
*WEWY??
*REALLY??
YEAH, IT WAS HONESTLY KINDA SCARY, YOU COULD PUSH ME ACROSS THE ROOM ALL BY YOURSELF.

*LIL' HERCULES...

Le Cray
BLACK
CHAPTER NINE
IN WHICH WE COME TO THE END OF OUR STORY
Samantha
Jacob

PRINCIPALS
SCHOOL WASN'T GETTING ANY BETTER FOR JACOB.
HE WAS HAVING SO MUCH TROUBLE, HE HAD TO GET HIS OWN PARA TO HELP HIM.
HI JACOB, I'M MISS SANDRA!
PLAY ALONG! GENTLY...
JACOB WAS **NOT** A FAN.
TOY STATION
ROOOAR! CRASH! AAAAAHHHHHH BOOOM!!
TOY STATION
OH JACOB, LET'S NOT BE SO **VIOLENT** WHEN WE PLAY...

TRY TO HOLD YOUR BODY STIL-
ACK!
SLURP!!
GO FLIP YOUR STICK!
RECESS IS OVER!! GET DOWN FROM THE TOWER!
NOW!!
WE HAVE TO COUNT THEM FIRST!!
I WANT IT!!
EVEN WITH A PARA, HE WAS STRUGGLING.
MM'S!!!

JACOB 5 MINUTES AFTER MEDICATION:

JACOB 20 MINUTES AFTER MEDICATION:

JACOB 60 MINUTES AFTER MEDICATION:

I HAD NEVER SEEN HIM SIT SO STILL BEFORE.
HIS ONLY MOVEMENT WAS TO TWIRL A SINGLE CURL AROUND HIS FINGER OVER AND OVER.
HE DID IT NONSTOP, EVERYWHERE HE SAT.
ALL THE TIME.
ANYWHERE.
HMM...?
OH, JACOB! YOU GAVE YOURSELF A BALD SPOT!!

YES, DOCTOR.
I SEE, THANKS FOR CALLING ME BACK.
THE DOCTOR SAYS IT'S NORMAL AND NOT TO WORRY...
APPARENTLY, A LOT OF KIDS WILL HAVE A TIC ONCE THEY'RE ON THESE MEDS.
I REALLY HATE PUTTING HIM ON MEDICIATION THAT MAKES HIM SO DIFFERENT...ARE WE MAKING THE RIGHT CHOICE...?
I'M JUST TRUSTING THE DOCTORS.
UGH!! BUT HE'S ALREADY DOING SO MUCH BETTER IN SCHOOL. HE MIGHT CATCH UP!

SIGHHH
I GUESS WE JUST WAIT AND SEE...

THERE WERE SOME POSITIVE THINGS ABOUT THE NEW AND STRANGE JACOB.
(A HAT TO KEEP HIM FROM PICKING)
Kitty!!
*WHAT AW YOU DWA-ING?
*WHAT ARE YOU DRAWING?
I'M INVENTING MY OWN ISLAND WHERE THESE SUPER SMART CATS HAVE THEIR OWN SOCIETY!
*CAN I DWAW TOO?
*CAN I DRAW TOO?
YEAH!!

LATER THAT NIGHT.

SAMANTHA, WAS THAT A HOMEWORK ASSIGNMENT YOU WERE WORKING ON EARLIER?
HMM?
OOH! CAT ISLAND. NO, THAT WAS FOR FUN!
DO YOU HAVE ANY FUN SCHOOL PROJECTS GOING ON?
OH YEAH, WELL, WE HAVE THIS ONE WHERE WE ARE DOING A HUGE FAMILY HISTORY TYPE THING–UH–WHERE WE GET UP IN FRONT OF THE CLASS AND TELL EVERYONE ABOUT SOMEONE IN OUR FAMILY WE ADMIRE. WE NEED PICTURES AND ART, AND I STILL HAVEN'T PICKED ANYONE.
I WAS WONDERING IF YOU WOULD HELP ME GO THROUGH OLD ALBUMS.
SURE THING, WHEN'S IT DUE?
UUHHHMM... TOMORROW...?

ARE YOU KIDDING ME??!!
SAMANTHA!!!!
I WAS GONNA WORK ON IT AFTER DINNER, I SWEAR! I'VE BEEN MEANING TO START IT, BUT I HAVEN'T HAD TIME!
WELL, HOW LONG HAVE YOU KNOWN ABOUT THE PROJECT?
UHHH, 3 WEEKS?
HEH HEH

OKAAAY...WHAT ABOUT-
THIS ONE! IT'S YOUR GREAT UNCLE MARK AT HIS WEDDING. MARK WAS THE PILOT FIGHTER IN WWII...
...HE'S THE ONE WHOSE PLANE WAS SHOT DOWN IN GERMANY.
EVERYONE IS DOING WAR STORIES, THAT'S WHY I WAITED...
...I WANTED TO PICK SOMETHING UNIQUE!
WHAT ABOUT THAT TIME YOU PEED YOUR PANTS AT THE ZOO!
DAD!!
HEY, HAHA LOOK AT THIS...

* A STORY ABOUT ME?

HERE'S A PICTURE FROM HIS FIRST EMERGENCY ROOM TRIP. REMEMBER HE SNUCK INTO THE KITCHEN AND TRIED TO CUT AN APPLE BY HIMSELF!
*OW DAT TIME I KNOCKET GABIN OUT OF DA TWEE WITH A BIG STICK!
WAIT, WHAT ABOUT A TREE?
NOTHING!!
*OR THAT TIME I KNOCKED GAVIN OUT OF THE TREE WITH A BIG STICK!
WE HAVE LOTS OF STORIES TO TELL ABOUT YOU, TINY TORNADO. I COULD WRITE A WHOLE BOOK!

I WANNA DO THIS ONE, FROM AUNT BETHANY AND UNCLE MIKE'S WEDDING!
IF YOU CHANGE YOUR MIND HALFWAY THROUGH...
GULP
FINISHED!!

OKAY, WE'LL RUN THROUGH IT A FEW TIMES, THEN STRAIGHT TO BED!
OKAY, HERE I GO! I'M STARTING!!
AHEM!
MY BROTHER JACOB IS A VERY UNIQUE BROTHER! ONE THING ABOUT JACOB IS...
...THAT HE'S NOT AFRAID OF ANY-THING! THIS MEANS HE GETS IN...
...TROUBLE A LOT, BUT IT ALSO MEANS HE'S VERY, VERY BRAVE!! LET ME TELL YOU A TALE...

My Brother Jacob

THE END

AUTHOR'S NOTE

While this story is a work of fiction, it is somewhat based on real shenanigans with my real brother, Jacob.

Real-life Jacob was also diagnosed as a young child with the neurodevelopmental disorder ADHD (Attention Deficit Hyperactivity Disorder). People with ADHD can present with one or a mixture of hyperactive, impulsive, and inattentive qualities that affect the way they navigate the world around them. The portrayal of ADHD in this book does not represent every person with ADHD, and it is not meant to be used as a diagnostic tool. It reflects the unique experiences I had with my brother from my point of view, and some of those things have nothing to do with ADHD; they're just pure Jacob-ness.

In Jacob's words: "I have always felt like I was popping in and out of reality, even during conversations. As a kid, I don't remember much, and that could be a result of ADHD. But I know I overcame my hyperactivity and my speech problems. And I remember that the people around me loved me despite me being a trouble-making tornado boy."

Those who grow up grappling with ADHD cope, explore, and enjoy life in their own unique way. Jacob's ADHD is part of what makes him a brave, hilarious, spontaneous, and exciting person. Without it, he wouldn't be Jacob.

When we were little, ADHD was not as well understood or even diagnosed the way it is today. Every day, we learn more about how kids with ADHD learn and the way their brains develop. If you have questions, you can learn more about ADHD at www.cdc.gov/adhd.

—Samantha

AUTHOR BIO

Samantha is a children's librarian and illustrator combo who lives in Kansas City, Missouri, with her two cats and husband. She loves cartoons, video games, comics, and all forms of visual storytelling.

ACKNOWLEDGMENTS

Many thanks to the various family, friends, and colleagues who supported me through this process:

To my parents, for letting me draw *Calvin and Hobbes* on my bedroom walls. To my library colleagues, especially Clare, for setting the stage. To my drawing teacher, Mark, for reigniting my love of comics. To my friends, Brooke and Jasmine, for lending me their talents and advice. And extra special thanks to my husband, Dr. Tucker, for providing in-house ADHD expertise and dragging my worn-out carcass over the finish line. Additional thanks to Lucas and those at AMU for giving me my first break.

Andrews McMeel Publishing
a division of Andrews McMeel Universal
1130 Walnut Street, Kansas City, Missouri 64106

21 22 23 24 25 SDB 10 9 8 7 6 5 4 3 2 1

ISBN: 978-1-5248-6504-7

Library of Congress Control Number: 2021935617

Editor: Lucas Wetzel
Art Director: Sierra S. Stanton
Production Editor: Jasmine Lim
Production Manager: Chuck Harper

www.andrewsmcmeel.com

Made by:
King Yip (Dongguan) Printing & Packaging Factory Ltd.
Address and location of production:
Daning Administrative District, Humen Town
Dongguan Guangdong, China 523930
1st Printing — 6/28/21